NO MORE WATER
IN THE TUB!

NO MORE WATER IN THE TUB!

Tedd Arnold

Dial Books for Young Readers New York

Published by Dial Books for Young Readers
A Division of Penguin Books USA Inc.
375 Hudson Street
New York, New York 10014

Copyright © 1995 by Tedd Arnold
All rights reserved
Design by Nancy R. Leo
Printed in Hong Kong
First Edition
1 3 5 7 9 10 8 6 4 2

Library of Congress Cataloging in Publication Data
Arnold, Tedd.
No more water in the tub!/Tedd Arnold.—1st ed.
p.   cm.
Summary: After filling the bathtub too full one night, William goes
sailing through his apartment building floor by floor in his tub,
collecting neighbors in his wake.
ISBN 0-8037-1581-1 (trade).—ISBN 0-8037-1583-8 (library)
[1. Baths—Fiction. 2. Humorous stories.] I. Title.
PZ7.A7379Nr 1995   [E]—dc20   93-33741   CIP   AC

The artwork was prepared using colored pencils and
watercolor washes. It was then color-separated and reproduced
as red, blue, yellow, and black halftones.

For William, who has waited so long,
and Walter, the best older brother
a boy could have.

In a bathroom near the top floor of a tall apartment building, William was ready for his bath. Walter had finished, and fresh water was running into the tub.

"Get in, William," said Mom. "Walter, keep an eye on your brother. Leave the faucet on another minute, then no more water in the tub!"

"Aw, Mom," William said as he climbed in. "I like it deep."

"You heard me. One minute." She closed the bathroom door as she left.

Walter reached for the tub faucet.

"Not yet!" William yelled.

"I'm turning it on faster," Walter answered, "so you'll get more water in one minute. Let's see how fast it'll go." He twisted the cold water handle and water gushed into the tub. "What if I turned it all the way until…"

it came off!

Water blasted out of the fixture.

In an instant the bathroom flooded. The tub broke loose and floated away from the wall. When Mom looked in to see what all the racket was, water burst through the door, taking the tub with it.

Down the hall William sailed, leaving Mom and Walter behind. Picking up speed, he passed the kitchen and the living room, heading for the front door. It opened.

"I'm home," said Dad.

Then out the door and down the steps went William in his bathtub.

In the apartment below, Miss Mabel Hattie was serving tea to her bridge club members when she heard a bump at the door. "That must be Betty at last," she said.

As Mabel opened the door, she complained, "Why are you always so late?"

But it was William who answered, "I didn't know you were expecting me."

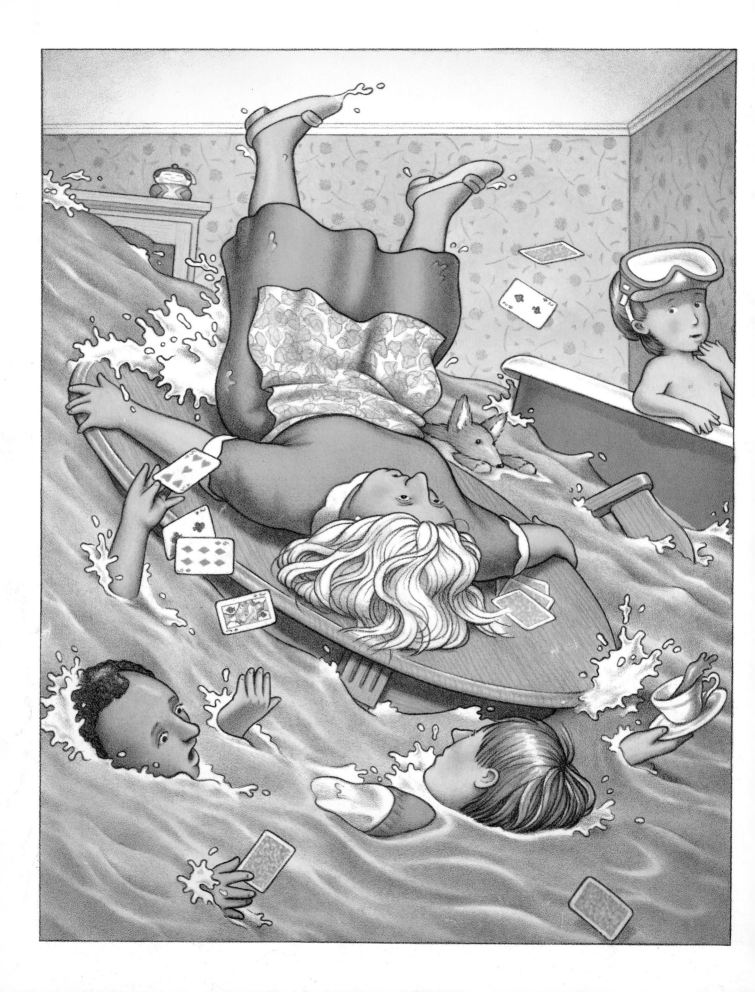

As a wave of water tipped Mabel backward, William rode his bathtub into the room. He circled the card table and followed the rushing waters back the way he came.

Then out the door and down the steps went William in his bathtub. Out went Mabel on the table.

One floor down, Sue and Vern Matty were watering their houseplants when they heard a knock. Expecting pizza to be delivered, Sue quickly answered the door.

"You're not our regular pizza boy," she sputtered as William surfed into the room, followed by Mabel. Waves rolled through the apartment, crashed against the back wall, and turned.

Then out the door and down the steps went William in his bathtub. Out went Mabel on the table. Sue and Vern clung to a fern.

Downstairs, Uncle Nash stepped into the hall to take out the garbage. He felt a drop of water and looked up. There was William, in a bathtub, plunging down a waterfall where the staircase used to be.

"I see your folks are having plumbing problems," Uncle Nash said as the churning water swept him off his feet.

Past the door and down the steps went William in his bathtub. Down went Mabel on the table. Sue and Vern clung to a fern. Uncle Nash sat in the trash.

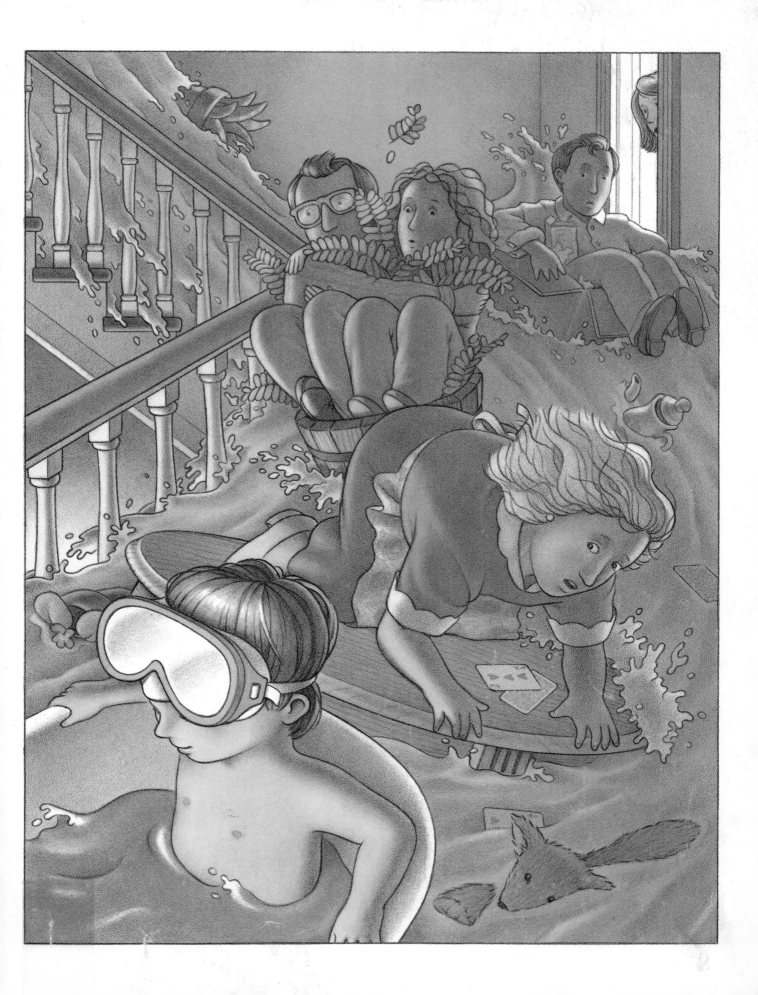

Patty Fuzzle was just about to put her last jigsaw piece into place. She heard a knock and thought her sister Natty was home from baby-sitting. But when she opened the door, it was William and the upstairs neighbors who spilled into the room.

"I have a sinking feeling I'll never finish my puzzle," she cried as the surging tide swirled her around.

Then out the door and down the steps went William in his bathtub. Out went Mabel on the table. Sue and Vern clung to a fern. Uncle Nash sat in the trash. Patty Fuzzle steered her puzzle.

    While Mr. and Mrs. Hanratty were out, Natty Fuzzle was baby-sitting little Dottie. They were in the bathroom, reading a story, when they heard a key in the front door.

    "That must be your mom and dad," said Natty. Then she heard water roaring down the hall toward the bathroom. William's tub pushed the Hanrattys inside. "We're home," they managed to say.

    Then out the door and down the steps went William in his bathtub. Out went Mabel on the table. Sue and Vern clung to a fern. Uncle Nash sat in the trash. Patty Fuzzle steered her puzzle. Little Dottie sailed the potty.

Downstairs, the Ferlingattis' string quartet had been practicing all evening.

"Mind if I fix a snack?" called Mr. Bellow from the kitchen.

"Make yourself at home," answered Mrs. Ferlingatti.

Suddenly the stove caught fire. Flames spread quickly.

"Call the fire department!" cried Mr. Bellow. "The building is burning!"

A fire alarm began to ring and everyone leaped to their feet. Mr. Bellow reached the door first and threw it open, yelling, "Run for your life!"

"But I just got here," said William. He and the neighbors stormed in on a tidal wave that flooded the burning apartment. Flames hissed. Smoke and steam filled the air. Just as quickly as the fire had started, it was gone and the water began draining away.

Then out the door and down the steps went William in his bathtub. Out went Mabel on the table. Sue and Vern clung to a fern. Uncle Nash sat in the trash. Patty Fuzzle steered her puzzle. Little Dottie sailed the potty. Mr. Bellow rowed his cello.

Fire trucks and crowds of people arrived as William clattered down the front steps of the building. The tub ran aground in the street and William's neighbors washed up behind it.

"Good work putting out that fire, son," said the fire chief. "You are a hero!" He hung a heavy medal around William's neck and everyone cheered!

"Then they all went home," Walter said. "The end!"

"That was a great story, Walter. Tell me another one!" begged William.

"Okay," said Walter.

William forgot all about turning the water off in one minute. The bathtub overflowed and quickly flooded the floor. Mom threw open the door and screamed, "No more water...!" But she was too late. The tub broke loose and floated away from the wall. Then out the window and down the fire escape went William in his bathtub....